MW00879939

Two-Inch Detective Finch's Tasty Mysteries

The Case of the Stolen Bikes

By L.J. Dunbar

Illustrated by Sophia Patch

GiaTia Press
Scottsdale, Arizona USA

The Case of the Stolen Bikes
Two-Inch Detective Finch's Tasty Mysteries

© 2019 L.J. Dunbar
All Rights Reserved
No portion of this book may be reproduced in any
form without express written consent of the author.

ISBN: 9781082078811

Illustrated by Sophia Patch

Published by GiaTia Press

Christmas 2020

This has been a hard & unusual year — But I know you have worked hard on your school work —

I hope you enjoy this fun book

We love you Nana & Papa

This book is dedicated to
my mother Rose Marlena.

Thank you for teaching me the
value and power of the written word.

Contents

1
Grandpa Finch's Shrinking Potion

T he day I opened that dusty, old box my life changed forever. It allowed me, 12-year-old Elias Alexander Finch, and 7th grader at Johnson Middle School, to become Two-Inch Detective Finch. A secret identity. It unlocked a world of tasty, new foods, excitement and danger.

Only a few people in this small, Iowa town knew about this. It all started when I found the box hidden in a corner of the basement while looking for my dad's old baseball cards. The words "Grandpa Finch's Potions" were written across the top in faded, black marker. Unable to contain my excitement, I tore it open.

You see, I already knew that my grandfather had experimented with mixtures he made from candy. Since he died when I was little, I couldn't ask him about what I had found.

But my father had explained a long time ago about the pink, purple and red fizzy liquids. Grandpa had poured the brews into paper cups and slurped them.

"A tall, thin man wearing yellow safety glasses and a white lab coat, he wiped dark curls away from his eyes and declared every sip delicious," my dad said.

According to my father, I look and act just like Grandpa. He has no idea how much!

Anyway, when I opened the box there were glass beakers, test tubes, small rusty pans and an electric double burner. I also found plastic bags full of red, blue, green, pink, purple, and yellow gummy bears, and tiny packets of Fizz Rocks candies.

My dad explained: "Each potion has a special purpose. Your grandfather scribbled the formulas into his little, black notebook. He always said someday these will work and do the world some good."

They never worked while Grandpa was alive but I've wondered if he could see into the future.

When he died my dad packed it all up into that box.

And now I held the book of potions. My fingers opened it slowly.

The notes printed neatly in pen were faded but I could read these three recipes...

To Make You Stronger

One cup club soda
Two grape gummy bears
One package of grape Fizz Rocks

Mix the club soda and Fizz Rocks together. When it stops fizzing and turns purple, take a slurp and eat a purple gummy bear. Close your eyes and wait two minutes. When you open them, you will be stronger. Take a second slurp and eat another purple gummy bear to reverse the potion.

To Sharpen Your Memory
One cup of club soda
Two cherry gummy bears
One package of cherry Fizz Rocks

Mix the club soda and Fizz Rocks together. When it stops fizzing and turns red, take a slurp and eat a red gummy bear. Close your eyes and wait two minutes. When you open them, your memory will be sharper. Take a second slurp and eat another red gummy bear to reverse the potion.

To Shrink to Two Inches Tall
One cup of club soda
Two cotton candy gummy bears
One package of cotton candy Fizz Rocks

Mix the Fizz Rocks and club soda together. When it stops fizzing and turns pink, take a slurp and eat one pink gummy bear. Close your eyes and wait two minutes. When you open them, you will be two inches tall. Take a second slurp and eat another pink gummy bear to reverse the potion.

Wow. I couldn't believe this. I wanted to shrink myself immediately. I grabbed a bottle of club soda from the upstairs refrigerator then pulled two pink gummy bears that smelled exactly like cotton candy from the plastic bags. I tore open some cotton candy Fizz Rocks and dumped them into a beaker with the club soda. The potion fizzed wildly and then a sparkling haze of smoke rose from the mixture. It turned hot pink and stilled. I held the glass to my lips and hesitated. My heart beat wildly. My stomach jumped. What would really happen if I drank this? Here it goes. I took a slurp. My taste buds tingled and came to life.

Yummmo. It's delicious like a sweet river of warm cotton candy flowing through me.

I cautiously touched the gummy bear to the tip of my tongue and gobbled it up.

MMMMMMMMM, tastes like a soft, fluffy cloud of cotton candy.

Feeling dizzy, I hobbled to a cot along the wall of the basement and lay down. Everything went black.

A few minutes later I opened my eyes and felt smothered in the heavy blankets. Frantically I kicked and screamed, trying to push off layers of something that trapped me.

I realized I had actually shrunk to two-inches and was buried inside my regular-size clothes. Was I dreaming? Then I heard footsteps and the basement door open.

"Eli, are you down there?" It was my dad.

"I'm here," I yelled as loud as I could but my voice was meek and soft. "Help me! I'm suffocating."

I heard my father run down the stairs and stop in front of the table where the pink liquid glowed like a beacon in the dark room.

"Noooo!" he screamed, choking on his breath. He pulled my jeans and shirt from on top of me. He stared at my naked body with a terrified look. I was the size of a flash drive. Then he yelled so loudly my mother and sister Gianna came bounding down the basement stairs.

"ELIAS ALEXANDER FINCH, I KNOW YOU FOUND THE BOX...BUT WHAT HAVE YOU DONE?"

I stood unsteadily on the cot, trying to balance in my new, tiny body.

My father ripped a square of toilet paper from a roll in the nearby bathroom, folded it in half, and wrapped it around me like a beach towel.

"AHHH," my mother let out a high-pitched scream. "Peter, what happened to Eli?" She clutched my father's arm.

My 7-year-old sister interrupted, "Cool

Eli. How did you get so small? You're cute. Can I put you in my dollhouse?"

"I drank Grandpa's shrinking potion," I squeaked in a tiny voice.

My dad shook his head. "How is this possible?"

He's an electrical engineer and doesn't believe in anything that can't be explained by logic.

"Why didn't those potions ever work for him and now they work...for you...?" he mumbled. "Did the ingredients become more potent as they aged over time? But that doesn't make sense. Maybe Eli is the one destined to use them."

My mother interrupted him and wailed. "Is this permanent?"

"Eli, is there a way to reverse the EFFECTS OF THE POTION?" Dad shrieked.

"I need to eat another cotton candy gummy bear and sip the pink liquid," I said.

My father snapped up a pink gummy bear and tore it into tiny pieces.

I nibbled it and swallowed.

He poured a drop of pink liquid into a cap from an eye drop bottle in his pocket.

I sucked it down my throat and breathed in. Sitting on the cot I closed my eyes. A hot liquid flowed through my body and shook it. My legs and arms stretched and pulled. I opened my eyes to see I was back to my normal size.

"Oh, thank goodness," my mom said clapping her hands. She quickly covered me with a sheet from the cot. "Don't EVER do that again!"

Dad continued shaking his head and mumbled something I couldn't hear.

Gianna sighed. "You won't fit in my dollhouse now."

An intense hunger like I'd never felt before overcame me. "I'm starved. What's for lunch Mom?" I clutched the sheet around my body, grabbed my clothes, and bounded upstairs.

2
Becoming Two-Inch Detective Finch

My mom forbade me to do it but I couldn't stop. I became an expert at shrinking. I spent the first few months using the potion to do everything as a two-inch-tall boy. I hid all over the house, crouched in kitchen cabinets, under sofa cushions, on shelves and behind things. It was like being invisible.

Soon I sneaked into candy shops, restaurants, cafeterias and grocery stores. Anywhere I could take a bite. Savoring the flavors, textures, smells, spices, sweetness, and tartness, I took in the richness of it all. I was a typical hungry teenage boy, but when

I shrank, my appetite grew out of control. I would do anything for food!

At Sally's Soda Shop on Main Street I sampled chocolate chip, mint chip, rocky road, birthday cake, raspberry sorbet, butter pecan and caramel swirl ice cream. I dipped my tiny fingers into the vats and licked off the soft, cold chunks.

MMMMMMMMMMMM. Smooth, creamy butter pecan... definitely the best. Soft and nutty, then that crunch makes it...soooo perfect.

I moved on to tasting candy. Jelly beans to be exact. Blueberry, chocolate, peanut butter, cherry, buttered popcorn and green apple. The morsels were tiny enough that when I jumped into the plastic drawers that held the beans, I could grab one and take a bite.

Cherry jelly beans are amazing, hands down. Chewy and soft like freshly picked fruit from the tree. Luscious and flavorful. I want more...

I also spent time doing something else I loved, reading. I was impressed with how *The Hardy Boys* solved so many mysteries. When I read *Harriet the Spy*, a story about a sixth grader who hid in people's homes, eavesdropped on conversations, and took notes about what she saw and heard, I had an idea.

It would be easy for me to spy on people. When I'm sooo tiny I can go anywhere unnoticed. I, Elias Alexander Finch, would solve mysteries by listening for clues. That same day I asked my parents to bring me to the town's police chief.

"Dad, I can help fight crime, follow

suspected criminals, eavesdrop on their conversations, and tell Chief Butterbeau what they said."

My dad looked shocked but then appeared to be thinking. Squishing up his face he said, "Your Grandpa Finch wanted his potions to do some good. He would approve!"

Mother said, "Absolutely not! It's dangerous. You could get smashed, stepped on, or eaten. No way!"

"Please mom. I promise to be careful!"

She was not convinced.

***

Chief Burton Butterbeau was tall and wide. He was also skilled at catching criminals. We had always heard that about him on TV.

"So, what can I do for you Peter?" he asked.

When my father slowly lifted my two-inch body out of his shirt pocket and placed me on the chief's desk, the officer nearly fell out of his chair. The color drained from his face as he stared at me.

"What the… That looks just like Elias! That's not possible!" He was shaking his head. "He's … no way, that's impossible!"

After Dad explained about Grandpa's miraculous shrinking potion, Butterbeau continued to stare at me.

"I can help you solve cases," my squeaky voice said. "Bad guys won't see me and I'll listen and tell you what they say."

"Well I'll be dipped," yelled Police Deputy Han Kuff from his desk across the room. "Look how little he is!"

My dad explained how the shrinking potion never worked for Grandpa but that Grandpa believed it would work one day and do some good. "Perhaps helping the police is the reason it worked for Eli," he told the officers.

***

As the school year began in the fall the chief focused on solving bigger crimes in town. I helped with small ones. On my first case I investigated a thief taking money from lockers at Anderson High School. This involved spending afternoons hiding in gym shoes and under smelly sweat socks inside the metal cubbies.

Before long student Jimmy Sallon broke into the very locker where I sat curled inside a sneaker holding my breath from the stench. He took $20 from a wallet.

When Chief Butterbeau brought him in for questioning he confessed.

"Good job solving your first case," the officer told me.

I was happy to help but longed to hide in food… not stinky shoes.

Speaking of terrible odors, in my next case I shimmied between gooey egg noodles in a tuna casserole while listening to two brothers plan a car heist. It was a close call and I was nearly scooped onto a plate by a serving spoon. And what a stink! I could barely keep from throwing up in the baking dish and getting caught.

The chief seemed surprised at how much information I remembered without writing it down.

Grandpa's *To Sharpen Your Memory* potion was the reason why.

"Your casserole caper helped us catch the worst car thieves this town has ever seen!" he said.

My hair smelled like dead fish for a week! Ewwww. But it was worth it to catch criminals.

"You're a great detective!" the chief told me. He awarded me with a police badge that looked just like a real one. *Two-Inch Detective Finch* was written on the front. That became the name of my secret identity.

When my dad saw the shield he grinned and said, "If Two-Inch Detective Finch is going to stay safe, he needs tools."

He fashioned ropes and ladders and tiny climbing carabiners for me. There was a miniature backpack, goggles, a helmet, and several pairs of shoes, including sneakers with wheels. He built a scooter and a cell phone for me to use if I ran into trouble. He also created two special suits. One was heat resistant, hooded coveralls for hiding in hot foods. The other was a wet suit for hiding in cold foods, like ice cream or my favorite chilled, cherry JELL-O.

For camouflage he used his 3D printer to make mini wraps I could stick on my clothes to look like food. One had a picture of spaghetti with tomato sauce on it so I could blend into the oversized, family-style pasta bowls at Fanelli's Diner. That one came in handy sooner than I had expected.

My mother was still against the idea of me being a two-inch tall detective but I knew she was softening because she sewed tiny jeans, coats, hats, gloves, sweaters, socks and underwear for me.

My parents allowed me to help with police business as long as I finished my homework and earned good grades in school.

3
Clues from the Spaghetti Bowl

I had heard enough as I shifted behind a plump meatball inside the enormous spaghetti bowl. I knew they were up to something. I had been in school with the twins, Mike and Matt Murphy, since kindergarten. They were 12 years old just like me and in my 7th grade homeroom. They had caused trouble over the years. And from the conversation I had just heard they were sure to be involved in the *Case of the Stolen Bikes*.

So, I parted the noodles, wiped a tomato off my goggles, and rolled off the backside of the deep dish. Nimbly, I braided three strands of pasta into a rope, wrapped one end tightly around my waist, and anchored the other under the Parmesan cheese shaker. As I rappelled to the floor, no one spotted me.

The restaurant was crowded with customers talking and laughing. All-You-Can-Eat-Spaghetti Night at Fanelli's Diner had waiters gliding through the room taking orders and delivering fresh, steaming-hot mounds of pasta and meatballs to the tables.

I bit off the yummy cord around my stomach to get free. I closed my eyes to savor Mr. Fanelli's cooking.

Mmmmm, delicious as always.

Zooming toward the exit on wheeled sneakers I hugged the walls to avoid getting stepped on. The weight of a child's shoe

could squish me like an ant. A man opened the door to enter the restaurant and I skated out. Ducking under a bush, I peeled off my wrap, heat suit and goggles. I stuffed them into a backpack on the handlebars of my electric scooter. I jumped on and headed home. It was dinnertime and the streets were empty. When I arrived in front of my house, I dialed Chief Butterbeau on my cell.

"It's Two-Inch Detective Finch reporting in," I whispered.

"What did you find out, son?" he asked.

I told him I had been inside the Murphy family's pasta and picked up some great clues.

But suddenly I was distracted...

Fanelli's spaghetti sauce was amazing. The blend of basil and garlic flavors were divine... and those fresh- simmered tomatoes slid so softly down my throat. Mmmmmmmmmmm.

I could eat it forever.

"Elias? Are you there?" The police officer sounded annoyed.

"Oh, sorry, yes. I saw the family's truck in the restaurant parking lot. So, I went home and shrunk myself, then sneaked into the diner. I spotted the table when I recognized the brothers' red and black sneakers from across the room."

The chief said he suspected the Murphy twins were stealing bikes. But he needed evidence; so, I was on the case.

"Were the boys' parents there? Butterbeau asked.

"Yes. I stayed behind the meatballs. Then I dodged the serving fork every time someone scooped up spaghetti. I tried not to get stabbed or swallowed."

"Detective work is a dangerous business," the officer said. "I'm glad you weren't hurt.

Every clue you gather is important to this investigation. If those trouble-making twins are stealing bikes, you can find out exactly what we need to prove it."

"Somebody stole my little sister Gianna's new, purple bike from our backyard today," I told him. "She's pretty upset. It was her birthday present. We went into the house to eat grilled cheeses for lunch, and when we came out it was gone."

I thought about my sandwich.

I love my grilled cheese on thick, sourdough bread with a slice of Swiss and slice of Cheddar melted over a single tomato into a soft mess. I stretch, then pull off gooey pieces and shove them into my mouth. They dissolve under my tongue.

"Including Gianna's that makes 10 bikes taken in two months," said the chief. "A few students at Anderson High School told me the twins were selling parts like pedals, mirrors, seats, and wheels for robotics projects. What did they say during dinner?"

"They have a lot of cash," I said. "And by the way, Fanelli's spaghetti was so tasty and the meatballs were tender with a hint of oregano, just delicious."

"Stop talking about food!" the officer snapped.

"Okay, Okay," I said. "Mike and Matt were whispering at the table so their parents couldn't hear, but I did. They talked about spending all of their money. They wanted to buy a basketball, candy, walkie-talkies and some new tools."

"I don't see how the boys would have the funds for those things," Butterbeau said. "Their dad Joe lost his job. Mr. Fanelli lets the family eat free on All-You-Can-Eat Spaghetti Night. And he employs their 17-year-old son Brian at the restaurant as a dishwasher."

"So where did they get the money?" I asked. "Are they stealing bikes?" I pushed my scooter under a shrub in the front yard, slipped into the house through the dog door, and headed for the basement.

"Good questions," the chief said. "I need you to do more investigating to find out."

With a two-man police department Butterbeau called in the county sheriff's department only for emergencies. Solving other crimes in town were left to him, his deputy – and now me.

"I'll do whatever it takes!" I said. And I meant it.

"Come to the station tomorrow morning and we can plan your next stakeout," he said.

"Sounds good," I told him and ended the call.

Quickly I reversed the shrinking potion and was back to my regular size. I pulled on jeans and a cotton shirt and dressed for dinner. As I ran up the basement steps toward the kitchen, I nearly crashed into my sister Gianna.

"Eli, where have you been?" she asked with hands on her hips. She pushed dark bangs from her eyes. "Were you looking for my bike? I want it back right now!"

"As a matter of fact, Gia, I was. I plan to find out who's stealing *all* the bikes." I told her what the chief had said about the other ones that were missing. "And don't worry, I'll get your birthday present back. But now I'm famished. What's Mom making for supper?"

We walked toward the kitchen where the smell of meatloaf wafted through the hallway. My thoughts followed the enticing scent.

Ahhh... soft, savory and spicy with bits of onions and green peppers inside those thick, beefy slices… a little barbecue sauce for dipping…I can't wait!

4
Just the Facts, Man

I decided to type the clues I'd gathered into notes and e-mail them to Chief Butterbeau. I needed to solve this case quickly. Gianna and the others deserved to get their bikes back.

My computer screen lit the dark room as my fingers moved swiftly across the keys. My stomach growled. I was hungry.

Hmmm... a PB&J with crunchy peanut butter and fresh blueberry fruit spread on soft, whole wheat bread. Each bite will stick to the roof of my mouth. Mmmmm.

I smiled at the thought, walked to the kitchen and grabbed the ingredients. I made a thick sandwich, sunk my teeth into it, returned to my desk with my plate and typed some more.

WHAT'S GOING ON WITH THE CASE?
SUSPECTS:

- Identical twins, Michael and Matthew Murphy, who live on Rivertree Lane with their mom, dad and older brother Brian, are suspected of stealing 10 bikes from Main Street, Johnson Middle School, Anderson High School and my backyard (Gianna's bike).

CLUES I HEARD HIDING IN SPAGHETTI:

- The brothers discussed splitting $300, and said they had to spend it fast. Why?
- Matt said he would buy candy, a tactical flashlight and remote-controlled toys.
- Mike said he wants a set of screwdrivers, computer parts and walkie- talkies so the

brothers can talk to each other during jobs. (I am not sure what he meant by jobs. Neither of them has a job. I never saw them working around town. In fact, I was used to hearing them talking in homeroom about how they needed money.)

- Mr. Murphy told the family that since he was laid off it is difficult to pay their bills. He asked Mike and Matt to mow lawns or help the neighbors with chores to earn some money. (The twins said NOTHING about the $300 they have. Not good.)

- Mrs. Murphy said she would sell embroidered dish towels and her *famous* chocolate chip cookies at bake sales to bring in some cash.

- Brian stopped by the table and said his salary working at Fanelli's would help with the family's expenses. This made Mike roll his eyes and whisper to his twin, "What a goody two-shoes!"

LOCATION OF BIKES? (Possible places the brothers would hide them.)

- In the old, abandoned barn behind the Murphy property?
- In the tall weed patch behind the canal?
- In abandoned railroad cars on the west end of town?

WHY STEAL BIKES?

- Chief Butterbeau says: "Every crime has a motive." In other words, there is a reason why people do bad things.
- Taking the bikes and selling the parts is a way for the twins to get spending money to buy what they want.

BACKGROUND ON THE MURPHY BROTHERS:

- The twins have been getting in trouble as long as I can remember. During 2nd grade gym class at Jackson Elementary School they put bubble gum in Judy Jesper's hair. Her mom had to cut it all out. She cried for weeks because big chunks of hair were missing and her pink scalp was showing.

- In 4th grade the boys freed their teacher Mr. Moffat's snake from its cage. The snake ate the 3rd grade's hamster. Miss Crabbons and her class were so upset about Hammy's death that the kids needed grief counseling.

- In 5th grade the twins brought a skunk to school and locked it in the principal's office overnight. When the school staff arrived in the morning the animal had sprayed such an awful stench through the building, school had to be cancelled for the day.

- The boys were expelled for this but their father talked Principal Allister into giving them another chance. Mike and Matt showed up with their dad. They wore their church suits and ties, their wild, red hair parted and perfectly combed. I heard they had apologized and were allowed to return to school.

I finished typing and hit the send button on my computer.

5
Here Kitty, Kitty!

I ate a big breakfast the next morning, blueberry pancakes with butter and maple syrup, crisp turkey bacon, and fresh-squeezed orange juice. I thought about it all the way to the police station.

Mmmmmmmmmmmmm. Hot blueberries popping in my mouth. Pancakes, thick and fluffy, drizzled with sticky brown sweetness and a hint of butter. The bacon's perfect crunch. The tartness of the oranges made my lips pucker.

By 9 a.m. I was at Butterbeau's desk ready for my next assignment.

40

"Excellent detective work in the notes you e-mailed me," he said. "I can always count on you. Today we need Two-Inch Detective Finch to do one more stakeout to confirm the twins stole those bikes. Then I'll bring them in for questioning."

I was thrilled.

"Let's start with your ideas about where the bikes may be hidden," he said. "The old, abandoned barn behind the Murphy property is a good place to check first. The roof is falling down and likely no one has been back there in years. For those reasons it's a great place to stash stolen goods. Why don't you have a look around? Go home, shrink yourself, and head over there to see if you find any bike parts. If the boys show up, listen for a while and report back to me."

***

An hour later I was two inches tall again. I also drank Grandpa Finch's *To Make You*

Stronger potion thinking I just might need it. A strange tingling sensation flowed through my body right after but I didn't feel any stronger.

It was like sipping from a flowing fountain of purple soda and then eating a mouthful of ripe grapes.

I dressed in jeans, a sweatshirt and my wheeled sneakers. I packed my cell phone, flashlight, ropes and goggles. Then I carefully wrapped tiny morsels of my favorite cheeses – Cheddar, Swiss, Pepper Jack and Colby. I zipped them into a pocket of my backpack knowing I'd be hungry while looking around the barn. I thought about how they would taste.

YUM. Bites of tangy Cheddar...a hint of hotness in the Pepper Jack ... that sweet, nutty

flavor of Swiss … and finally, the softer, lighter
sensation of Colby. In my mouth they're like
popcorn and they melt nicely on my tongue.
Heavenly!

I slipped quietly out of the house through
the dog door trying to avoid my Labrador
retriever Sandy. She was sprawled across
the upstairs hall on her back, asleep. She
often grabbed me by the collar and carried
me around like a chew toy. How annoying!
There was no time for that.

My scooter was still hidden behind
the shrub from the night before. I hopped
on unnoticed. A winding dirt road ran
alongside and behind the Murphy home
leading to the old barn. I drove right in since
the front doors were missing. It took a while
to check the structure because the roof
was falling and chunks of rotted wood and

debris littered the floors making it difficult to navigate. No sign of bikes or the twins but I was sure they were close by.

Then I heard a rustling noise in a pile of wet hay. I turned quickly to face four gigantic towers of hairy, black fur.

"Meowwwwwww! Eeeeeoooowwww... eeeeeoooowwww...."

The sound echoed eerily through the barn.

A black cat loomed over me like a mountain lion. Its teeth shone sharp and fierce. The pink tongue taunted me. Before I could react, the animal whacked me with its front paw. Its pads were triple my size and like a large curtain, kept out all the light.

"Whoaaaaaaaa..." I flew off of the scooter and slid across the filthy floor. My backpack clung tightly to my shoulders and broke my fall. It kept me from getting injured. Dizzy and terrified I dashed across the room.

Panting, my heart racing, I imagined being chewed alive like a tiny mouse.

"Meowwwwwww! Eeeeeoooowwww… eeeeeoooowwww…."

The cat chased me and its paw came down and slapped me again. This time I flew into the air and across the barn. With a thud my body landed in a crack between two loose floorboards. I sneezed from the thick dust. Terrified in the pitch black I tried to calm myself and think. I was digging through my backpack for something to distract the cat… and save myself. What can I use? Found it!

"Here kitty, kitty. Come on kitty," I yelled. "You're gonna love THIS!"

The cat scampered over and looked curiously down the crack. It clawed at the opening but the gap between the boards was too narrow to reach me. I slowly unwrapped my precious bits of Swiss, Cheddar, Colby and Pepper Jack knowing they were my

lifelines out of the barn.

The cat sniffed and then clawed at me. Thanks to Grandpa's *To Make You Stronger* potion I was able to heave a chunk of Colby clear across the barn, followed by a nugget of Swiss… and then Pepper Jack.

After each toss, the beast tore after the cheese, gobbled it up and quickly trotted back to my hiding place and licked its chops.

There was no time to escape. I saved the shard of Cheddar for last because it was my favorite. It had to work or this was the end for me.

I studied the barn from my hiding place and noticed some large bales of hay piled up in a corner. The top one teetered. If I can throw the Cheddar right there on that unstable haystack the cat will jump on it to get the cheese and fall. I aimed that final morsel and flung it.

The cat took the bait and leaped. I wasted

no time getting out of that crack as the cat, the hay, and the cheese tumbled several feet to the floor.

"RAAAAAAWWW….aaaaawwww…. aaaaawwww!"

It was a deafening screech.

Then silence.

I dashed across the floor to my scooter and accelerated out the door. When I looked back one last time the cat was lying down licking itself. My only regret was not saving any cheese. I was starving.

I turned the corner and noticed a large root cellar next door. Bingo. Now *this* would be the perfect place to hide some bikes!

6
Just Peachy

When I reached the cellar, I felt an uneasy chill. Goosebumps spread over my body. I was on the verge of discovering something. Tossing my scooter in some nearby brush I walked toward the door. I squeezed through a gap under the solid wood entry. Using a rope, I climbed down the broken stairs.

The room was quiet and smelled musty. A dingy light bulb dangling from a few wires barely brightened the space.

Then I saw them. Stacked in a corner were 10 bike frames stripped of wheels, mirrors, pedals, seats and the rest of their parts. Gianna's purple birthday present poked out from the bottom of the heap.

"Those rotten thieves!" I moved closer to get a better look. I needed to call Chief Butterbeau but instead I just stood there shocked that I had found them.

By the time I pulled out my cell Mike and Matt's voices resonated through the cellar.

I spied a tall shelf lined with glass jars caked with dirt and thick cobwebs. I lassoed one of the containers with my rope. Grandpa Finch's *To Make You Stronger* potion helped me hoist my body up there. I dodged behind the row just as the brothers entered the cellar. Now, tangled in a blanket of cobwebs, it was impossible to spot me.

The twins stood over the pile of metal.

"What are we doing with these bike frames now that we sold off all the parts?" Matt asked. "I mean, we can buy cool stuff with the money, but don't you think someone will tell the police chief we sold the wheels and mirrors at Anderson High School?"

Mike dragged his right hand through his red hair until a clump was almost standing up. I saw him do this same thing at school when he was taking a test.

"Well, I think we have enough money now so we won't need to steal more bikes," Mike said. "We can just bury them behind the barn. No one will look out here. And if anyone asks us about them, we just say we don't know anything about it."

Matt gave his brother a questioning look. "I guess," he said. "But burying all of these will take a long time. What if someone sees us?"

"We have to do it at night," said Mike. "And we need to scatter them around the property so we don't have to dig big holes."

"That'll take forever," Matt said. "Maybe we should ask Brian to help us. That will make it quicker."

"No way," said Mike. "He'll tell Mom and Dad for sure. He's always sucking up to our parents and bossing us around. You better not tell him a thing!"

Matt sighed. "Ok, well, I guess we'll need some shovels."

"We'll get Dad's tools from the garage once he's gone," Mike said. "He'll be out all day tomorrow looking for a job. We can come back here as soon as it's dark."

"Do you really think this is going to work?" Matt asked. "I mean that we won't get caught?"

"Don't worry," said Mike. "Once we bury the bikes no one will ever know we did it."

Once the brothers left, I used my phone to call the chief. "I found the bikes!" I screamed into the phone. "They're in a cellar behind the Murphy house. Mike and Matt were here and said they'll bury the frames tomorrow night before anyone finds them!"

"Great work son!" Butterbeau said. "I figured they were close to the property. Are all 10 bikes there?"

"Yep."

"Good. Don't touch anything and come back to the station," he said. "I'll bring the boys in for questioning and ask the parents' permission to search the cellar. Then Deputy Kuff will pick up the bikes."

"Ok, it's just east of the barn off the dirt road," I said.

After I ended the call my stomach growled furiously. It had been hours, but felt like days, since breakfast and I had used all my cheese to stop the cat from eating me!

There had to be something here. After all, don't people use their root cellars to store food? Then I realized the jars where I was hiding had something edible in them. But what?

I wiped layers of dirt from a single jar for what seemed like forever. Then finally I glimpsed the treasure inside. It was golden chunks of peaches preserved perfectly. My mouth watered and taste buds tingled. The peaches seemed to be begging me to taste them.

Yum, soft and silky... all melted and warm dissolving on my tongue. It reminds me of Mom's peach cobbler. The peaches are sweet and tender. The crust is crunchy. The insides gooey. Top it off with vanilla ice cream and a dollop of whipped cream.

I had to find a way into that jar. So, I tied my rope around it, rappelled to the ground, and yanked it hard. I wanted the impact of the fall to rupture the glass and expose my treats. Success. It hit the floor and broke cleanly in half. Without wasting time, I dipped my finger into the golden, syrupy nuggets.

I had no idea a second jar that was also dislodged wobbled on the edge of the shelf. Then I heard something smash on the floor. Only this time the bottom half of the glass rolled and landed on top of me. I hadn't seen it coming because my eyes were closed as I savored that first bite.

Now I was trapped inside a capsule of slimy, scrumptious peaches. The air was thin and the mess hardened around me. A small sliver of glass had broken out near my face, allowing me to breathe, but I couldn't budge. I was up to my chin in peaches.

Ugh. I squirmed trying to push out my arms and legs. I fought against the muck until I was exhausted. Then I surrendered. The pleasant aroma of fruit finally released from its glass container after years overcame me. My breathing slowed. I inhaled deeply, taking in the unique deliciousness. Once my mind had cleared, I knew exactly what to do.

Eat peaches! Lots of them. If I swallowed enough chunks from around my body, I could free my arms, push off the glass and save myself. So, I shoved my face into the golden mess and got busy. After every few bites I pulled my head up, took a breath, dove back in and kept right on chewing. And chewing. I knew one thing for sure, if I survived this, I would NEVER eat another one of these things again!

Finally, I freed my right arm from the mountain of goo but my belly was stuffed. I rocked the jar slightly but not enough to tip off me.

I kept pushing until I was spent. The cell phone in my left pocket, along with my left arm, was still stuck. So, calling anyone was out of the question.

For the first time, *food* – that wonderful, tasty, yummy, amazing thing I loved most in the world that had protected me and

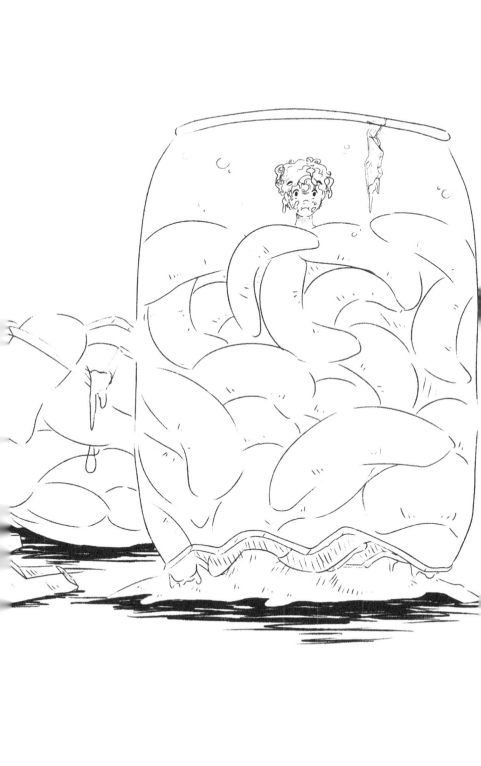

was essential to my detective work—had become the enemy.

Those delicious peaches had almost killed me! The gunk coating my face and hair had hardened. I could barely open my eyes. But I tried to be positive.

I could be stranded in a sea of hot fudge swimming to safety... or in a mound of macaroni and Cheddar cheese. I would fashion the noodles into steps to escape. Or I could dig my way out of a river of jelly beans... eating the cherry ones first...then the root beer... yum, yum.

Light flashed across the room as the cellar door opened. Deputy Kuff bounded down the stairs and stopped right in front of me.

"What the heck are you doing?" he yelled. He flipped over the glass and yanked me out with his thumb and forefinger.

"I was hungry," I said. "Thanks for rescuing me. I was beginning to think I'd become a permanently bottled peach."

The officer handed me a folded tissue. After peeling off my stained clothes I wrapped it around me like a cloak.

"So, this is what they did with the bikes," he said, looking over the stack. He put on gloves and carefully dusted each for fingerprints, picking up several images with square tape. Then he loaded the frames into his truck. "Those boys can't stop getting into trouble," he said. "I wonder what the judge will do with them. I think Chief Butterbeau has a plan to teach them a lesson!"

He dropped me off at home and said to meet him at the police station later that afternoon.

It took me a while to scrub off all the debris in a hot shower. Yet a faint, sweet peach odor lingered after I dried off. The smell of Mom's chicken pot pie quickly overcame it. I inhaled deeply and thought about it.

MMMMMM, pieces of white meat chicken in a savory cream sauce with soft carrots, peas and potatoes... and that crunchy, buttery, perfectly-browned crust. I can't live another day without a piece.

7
The Brothers' Grim

O n the way to the police station I spotted Mike and Matt walking into Bentley's Department store on Main Street. Of course, I followed them. I stayed several paces behind even though I was my regular size. They were absorbed in their shopping spree and didn't notice me.

At checkout I saw they purchased computer parts, candy bars, walkie- talkies, sports equipment, flashlights, a set of screwdrivers and some remote-controlled toys.

After they left, I decided to go home, shrink myself, and sneak into the Murphy house to wait for Chief Butterbeau to show up and bring them in for questioning.

***

At the house I hoisted myself through an open guest room window on the second floor. The next room over was the twins' bedroom. I slipped under their door and hid in a pile of dirty clothes in the corner of the room.

Phew... it stunk, but I could peek out and see everything. Bunk beds and two desks occupied one side of the room. The rest of the space was filled with projects.

Mike added the circuit board he just bought to a robot he was building. He also used wheels and reflectors, I guessed, from the stolen bikes. Parts were scattered everywhere.

Matt flew a remote-control helicopter and crash-landed it on the beds. He stopped to tear open a box of candy bars.

"I love these things," he said and closed his eyes as he bit into one and chewed slowly.

When I heard the familiar sound of squeaky brakes on Butterbeau's police car I knew he had arrived.

"The police chief is here," Mike said in a panicky voice as he looked out the window.

Matt dropped the chocolate.

"Hide your stuff," Mike said, as both boys tidied the room, moving the new purchases out of sight. Mike shoved a basketball and walkie-talkies under the bottom bunk.

"He knows what we did," Matt said, sounding scared. "Why do I let you talk me into these things!"

"Don't worry. We'll come up with something to tell him," said Mike. "Besides, look at all the cool stuff we bought! And we spent all $300 so we can't give it back." He smiled.

"Do you think we'll go to jail?" Matt

asked. He rubbed his hands together like he was trying to warm up.

"Nah, we're too young," his brother said.

I heard the officer talking to the twins' mom in the kitchen.

The boys finished cleaning up, grabbed some schoolbooks, and sat at their desks to look like they were studying.

I tiptoed under their door, slid down the stair banister, sneaked into the kitchen and hid behind the refrigerator.

"Good afternoon, Chief," Lora Murphy said with a smile. "What can I do for you? Joe is out looking for work right now if you came to see him. How about a cup of coffee and some chocolate chip cookies?" She offered him the platter.

Chief Butterbeau nodded.

How could he resist one of her *famous* chocolate chip cookies?

A memory flooded my mind.

Mrs. Murphy's chocolate chip cookies…
soft, thick and chewy… melting in my mouth.
She makes the best ones in the universe… with
giant, dark and white chocolate chips. Sweet!

The officer plucked a large one off the plate and bit into it. Then he broke the news. "Do you know why I asked your permission to search the root cellar behind your house?" he asked.

"Not really. I was wondering but assumed it was something routine," Mrs. Murphy said.

"We retrieved 10 bicycle frames from there and I believe your sons may know where they came from. I'd like to take them down to the police station for a few questions."

Her face lost its color and she sat down at the kitchen table.

He continued, "A store clerk has a receipt that says your boys spent $300 at Bentley's Department store this afternoon."

"Where did they get that kind of money?" she asked.

"Students at Anderson High School told me they purchased some bike parts from the twins for robotics projects. And a witness heard the boys talking about burying the frames on your property."

Lora Murphy frowned. "I've been so busy helping Joe find jobs, baking, and sewing things to sell, that I haven't paid attention to what the twins have been into," she said, wiping away a tear. "I can't believe this. What happens to them if they did this?"

"Since they're young, and this was the first time they've committed a crime, they'd have to do some community service," Butterbeau said. "I have some ideas. I'll talk to you and Joe after I question them. Okay?"

She went upstairs looking upset and a few minutes later the twins trailed behind her and into the kitchen.

"You boys need to come down to the station to answer questions about the bikes we found in your cellar," the officer said.

The brothers gave each other a brief, shocked look, silently followed him out, and climbed into the back of the police vehicle.

8
Confessions and Diversions

I arrived at the police station back at my regular size. Deputy Kuff said Mike and Matt had already been fingerprinted and ushered into an interview room.

"I smell peaches," he teased.

"I can't get that odor out of my hair," I told him. "By the way, thanks again for saving my life."

"You were in quite a pickle," the deputy said laughing, "or should I say a peach!"

The chief overheard us talking as he came out to get the twins some water before questioning them. He gave us both a stern look.

"This is no laughing matter. That was a close call, Elias, and you could have been killed. Trying to eat an old jar of peaches and getting stuck in it. That's a first. You need to control your appetite! We've had this conversation before."

"But I love food…I can't stop thinking about eating." I said.

As the chief continued to lecture me, I tuned out. I had already forgotten my vow to strike peaches from my life and thought of all the delicious foods that could be made with them:

Let's see, there's peach crisp, frozen peach pops, peach pound cake, grilled peaches with a honey glaze, peach cookies, peach cupcakes with cream cheese frosting, peach caramel pie, peach scones, peach ice cream, peach jam, peach pancakes, peach lemonade, peach fruit leathers, peach green tea, peach yogurt, peach shortbread, peach jelly beans…

"Elias! Are you listening!" he snapped.

"Yeah… my parents are pretty mad too," I said. "They told me I needed to be more careful and I have to stop munching on everything. I hope I can keep doing detective work."

Since everyone was so upset, I decided it was best NOT to mention the encounter with the barn cat or that I would have died there too if it weren't for my creative cheese choices.

"I'll talk to them," Butterbeau said. "You did a first-rate job on this case. The twins will be dealt with, and I'll let your parents know how valuable you are to the police department."

"Thanks. I appreciate it," I said. "And

what will happen to Gianna's bike?"

"You'll find out soon," he said and walked toward the interview room to speak with the brothers.

I followed him and stood outside watching through the one-way glass. My side of the window was transparent and their side was a mirror. I could see and hear them but they were unaware of me.

The chief began with a scowl, looking from one brother to the other. "We found each of your fingerprints on the bike frames you hid in the cellar behind your house. Deputy Kuff brought them to our evidence room. What do you have to say?"

Beads of sweat formed on Matt's forehead. His face flushed and he stared at the floor. Then he spoke up. "It was Mike's idea…he talked me into it. I really didn't want to do it."

"What happened?" asked Butterbeau,

his angry voice rising.

Mike ran a hand through his wild hair and remained silent.

Matt continued, "I was the lookout making sure no one saw when Mike grabbed each bike and rode away. None of them were locked up. No one even noticed what we were doing."

"Did you steal 10 bikes?" the officer said gruffly. Suddenly, he was nose to nose with Mike.

Mike moved his face away, breaking eye contact with the chief, and whispered, "Yes, are we going to jail?"

The room went silent until Matt chimed in again. "We took the bikes behind our house, stripped off parts and sold them, mostly to high school kids. Mike also used some for his robot."

"I know you spent $300 in town today," Butterbeau said, "buying candy and toys. Is that how much you made on the bikes?"

The twins nodded.

The officer cleared his throat and said, "What were you thinking? Your family needs you to step up and earn money to help with the bills. This is a tough time for your father. You're both bright and clever. Why not use your brains to do something that is NOT illegal!"

"We didn't hurt anyone," Mike said. "We just took a few bikes."

"Petty theft is a crime," Butterbeau said. "You broke the law. Have you considered how you hurt the people whose bikes you stole? Every criminal act causes harm, in more ways than you know."

The brothers stared at the floor.

The chief still looked annoyed. "Since this is your first offense you qualify for the Iowa Youth Services Diversion Program. That means completing community service and classes to keep you out of court and from getting a criminal record."

Mike gave Butterbeau an angry glare.

Matt nodded.

"I'll talk to the judge and bring you back here tomorrow to sign your contracts," he said. "I hope these consequences will convince you to NEVER steal again!"

When their father arrived at the station the brothers did not say a word or make eye contact with him.

As they walked out the door he bellowed, "This is the LAST thing I need right now."

Without a word the boys slowly climbed into the cab of his rusty, old pickup truck.

***

The next morning, I was back at the police station watching through the one-way glass as the twins and their parents signed the Iowa Youth Services Diversion Program contracts in the interview room.

"If each of you completes what's listed here your cases will be dismissed," the chief said. "If you don't, you'll wind up in Juvenile Court."

He handed each twin an identical contract and read the key points:

- Attend and pass a Crime Prevention class at Juvenile Court.
- Community service work after school and on weekends for six months at Higley's Bike Repair Shop.
- Repair all 10 stolen bikes and hand them back to their owners in person.
- Return all items purchased with the $300 gained from selling the parts.
- Use the $300 to purchase new parts for the stolen bikes.

The twins and their parents agreed and everyone signed the contracts. Joe and Lora Murphy stepped out of the room to talk with the chief, leaving the twins alone.

I heard Mike say, "What a bummer we can't keep the stuff. I need that circuit board for my robot."

"Are you serious?" Matt snapped. "We're lucky we won't get a criminal record. I never wanted this. The pranks we did in elementary school are one thing, but stealing is a new level of bad."

Mike rolled his eyes and said, "Stop overreacting. It's no big deal."

9
Rebuilding Bikes and Lives

Mr. Higley opened his bike repair shop every morning exactly at 8:30 a.m. He wore a red, starched apron over a white shirt and black dress pants. His leather shoes were buffed so clean you could see yourself in them.

But this morning was different. Instead of opening his door he dropped by the police station to collect the names and phone numbers of the stolen bike owners. Since each had filed a police report the chief had their information.

I was at the station and heard Mr. Higley

tell Butterbeau how surprised he was that the twins worked so quickly. "They have already rebuilt all 10 bikes," he said.

That meant it was time for Mike and Matt to return them.

"I hope having to face the owners will change the twins' attitudes," the chief said.

My sister Gianna's purple birthday bike was first on the list. I wanted to be there as Two-Inch Detective Finch to see this.

"Why don't you hide in a candy machine at the shop," Butterbeau suggested. "Let me know how it goes."

"I can taste the delicious snacks right now," I answered.

"Don't get carried away eating sugar," he warned. "You're supposed to be working."

I was out the door and on my way home to shrink myself.

***

I sneaked into the repair shop that

afternoon wearing goggles and my heat resistant coveralls. Using ropes, I hoisted myself onto the old-fashioned candy dispenser, pulled up the lid, and jumped in. The crystal bowl was in the center of the room and gave me a perfect view. It had been in the bike shop as long as I could remember. Only a quarter would buy you a handful of red, hot treats. I inhaled the spicy, cinnamon scent and felt dizzy.

"This bike belongs to Gianna Finch," Mr. Higley told Mike and Matt.

"We know who she is," Mike said and shot Matt a quick glance. "Her brother Elias is in our class."

Through the window I saw my mom waiting outside and then Gianna walked in. She wore her pink birthday dress and ballet shoes to celebrate the reunion with her bike.

She grabbed the handlebars and giggled. Then she hugged it like a long-lost friend.

When she let go, she glared at the twins. "WHY did you steal my brand-new bike?" she asked. "You ruined my birthday and made me cry. I hardly got to ride it. You're so mean and I hate you!"

"I'm sorry," said Matt. "We...we…"

"We wanted some money," Mike interrupted.

"That's just wrong," Gianna declared. She took her prized possession and walked right out the door.

Inside the candy dispenser I cheered for her but no one heard me.

The brothers watched until she was out of sight and then continued working in silence.

While waiting for the next person to arrive I dove head first into the red-hot candy heap. The smooth beads covered my body but they didn't burn me because of the heat resistant coveralls. I turned onto my back, placed a morsel in my mouth, and savored the fiery flavor burst.

Ohhhh so zesty, yet sweet… like eating a fireball with a crunch then a chew, then dousing the flame with cinnamon. I want some more!

"Harley Johnson is coming to get that red and silver Schwinn GTX sports bike," Mr. Higley announced.

"Glad we don't know him," Matt whispered to his brother. "He must live in the next town."

A tall, dark-haired boy came in the shop, smiled broadly at his bike, and grabbed it. "I've been training to compete in the Corn Husk Race," he said frowning at Mike and Matt. "It only comes around every two years. I was a top pick to win but you stole my bike the night before the race. I had to forfeit! Now, I have to wait two more years to compete. You guys are jerks!"

"We didn't mean to…" Matt stuttered.

Mike tried to interrupt again but Harley shoved his Schwinn ahead of him, left the shop, and slammed the door behind him.

Just then Mr. Bentley, owner of Bentley's Department store, marched in. "I'm here to collect the five bikes you took from the display in front of my store," he said sharply. "You should be ashamed of yourselves."

He towered over the twins and wagged a finger in their faces. "These were brand new Beach Cruisers for people to BUY! NOT FOR YOU TO STEAL! Now you've torn them up and put them back together like Frankenstein. I consider them used."

"But we bought new parts and put them on," Mike countered.

"I don't care," yelled Mr. Bentley. "I'm going to tell Chief Butterbeau to make sure you two pay me back every penny with interest on whatever profit I lost on these!"

"I'm really sorry Mr. Bentley," Matt said.

He looked like he was going to cry.

"Me too," said Mike.

But he was smiling and didn't seem sorry to me.

Mr. Bentley ignored them, loaded the bikes into his shiny, black pickup truck, and zoomed off without another word.

10
Turning It Around

I left the shop with a tummy ache from eating too much candy.

"The twins have returned seven bikes so far," I told Chief Butterbeau on the phone that night. "I'm glad Mr. Bentley yelled at them but I feel sorry for the kid who missed his chance to compete in the Corn Husk Race."

"I hope when those boys realize the far-reaching impact of their bad choices, they'll turn away from crime," the officer said.

***

The next day I hid in a more modern candy vending machine at the repair shop. I was craving sugary snacks again.

I slipped through the front door after a customer had left. Squeezing under the main dispenser flap and using my ropes, I climbed up. Hunkered behind a king-size chocolate bar, I blended in perfectly.

The delightful smells overpowered me. There were chocolate wafers, mints, cookies, chips, cheese puffs, peanuts, gum and chocolate-coconut candy with almonds. If the twins took their time returning bikes, I'd have a chance to taste it all. I popped a piece of deliciousness in my mouth and my thoughts drifted.

The way this chocolate melts on the tip of my tongue is intense...milky with a perfect sweetness.

Mr. Higley announced that Jent Homer, who looked a little older than I am, was here

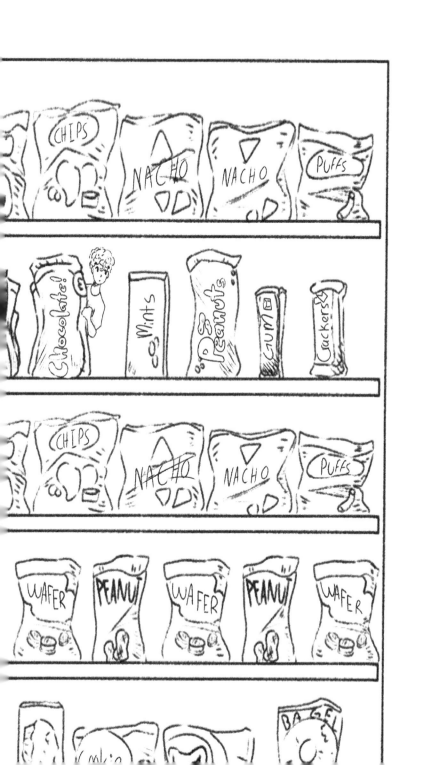

to pick up his blue Beach Cruiser.

To the twins he said, "I was supposed to help some elderly friends fix a hole in their roof. But I couldn't get there because you took my bike. There was a thunderstorm and water poured in. It ruined their carpet and furniture. And it's all your fault."

"Oh, my gosh," Matt said. "I feel terrible. What can we do?"

"Never mind," Mike interrupted. "We can't help if it rained!"

Jent took his bike and left the store looking sad.

I moved lower in the vending machine to a clip that held the chocolate- coconut candy bars with almonds. I tore the wrapper, twisted off a piece and positioned it on my tongue. I closed my eyes and savored it.

I just can't get over the way the coconut and chocolate blend in my mouth with the crunchy

almond, creating a symphony of flavors. My
tongue is tingling with joy...almondy joy.

Haleigh Hills, a sophomore at Anderson High School, came into the shop to pick up her yellow, Huffy Cruiser. A cute girl with long brown hair, she wore ripped jeans, a T-shirt and worn-out tennis shoes. She knew the twins and wasn't shy about her feelings.

"Thanks to you two I lost my waitress job at The Coffee Cup," she declared as she ripped her bike from Matt's grip. "My mom is sick and her car broke down. I rode to work every day after school. After you guys stole my bike I was always late for work because it took too long to walk there. So, my boss fired me!"

"We've hurt so many people. I feel awful you lost your job because of us," Matt said.

Mike nodded.

"I'll figure things out," she said. "Now that I have my bike maybe I can get my job back." Then she left.

I had a close call when someone put quarters in the vending machine and a package of peanuts came flying down, grazing my left ear. I moved my head sideways just in time. I could have been killed!

"I can't do this anymore," Matt said. "It's too hard!

"I never thought all this could happen from taking a few bikes," said Mike.

"One more and you're done," Mr. Higley said. "Here comes Amy Miller."

The boys gave each other a surprised look. Amy Miller was their 7th grade classmate at Johnson Middle School.

"Ugh," said Matt. "She's going to hate us!"

The twins had stolen Amy's bike from the middle school parking lot.

Her long, chestnut hair flowed over her shoulders. Crying, she came into the shop to retrieve her yellow Huffy.

"Oh … why did you guys steal my bike?" she said. "My grandmother might die because of you!"

"What?" asked Matt. "I can't take another sad story."

"Every day after school I rode my bike to the nursing home to see her. After you took it, I couldn't get there because my mom was at work. My grandmother was so upset that I wasn't coming to see her that she stopped eating. The people at the nursing home said she's drinking liquids but she'll die if she doesn't eat food soon!"

Matt cried too and said: "Can you ever forgive us? Your poor grandmother. How can we help?"

Mike shook his head. "I'm sorry we stole all the bikes. I had no idea. We just wanted to buy a few things."

"This is a mess," Matt said. "Amy, we'll build you a better, faster bike. Somehow, we'll pay all these people back."

"After this community service ends, we'll earn money to help our family with bills too," Mike said.

I stopped eating and tears glistened in my eyes. I was relieved to see *The Case of the Stolen Bikes* was closed, and that the twins might finally stop causing trouble – at least for now. I slipped out the door and headed back to the police station, hungry for my next tasty investigation.

Two-Inch Detective Finch's Favorite Recipes

 ## Gooey Grilled Cheese

(serves 1, but recipe can be doubled)

Ingredients

- 2 teaspoons softened butter
- 2 thickly-sliced pieces of sourdough bread
- 1 slice Swiss cheese
- 1 slice Cheddar cheese
- One thick, large tomato slice

Directions

1. Spread half of the butter over one side of each bread slice.

2. Put one slice, butter side down, on work surface. Add Swiss, the tomato slice, then Cheddar; cap with remaining bread, butter-side up.

3. Melt some butter in skillet over medium heat. Cook sandwich, turning once, for about 5 minutes or until bread is golden brown and cheese is melted and covers tomato.

4. Let cool, then devour.

Yummo PB&J

(serves 1, but recipe can be doubled)

Ingredients

- 1 tablespoon crunchy peanut butter
- 2 tablespoons blueberry spread (get the kind with fruit chunks in it)
- 2 slices of soft, whole wheat bread

Directions

1. Spread crunchy peanut butter on one side of a slice of bread and fruit spread on one side of the second slice.

2. Slap the covered sides together.

3. Sink your teeth into the sandwich and take a large bite.

Mom's Old-Fashioned Peach Cobbler (serves 6)

Ingredients

- ¾ cup granulated sugar
- 2 tablespoons all-purpose flour
- ½ teaspoon salt
- ½ teaspoon cinnamon
- ½ teaspoon allspice
- 1 ¾ pounds peaches (20 pieces) canned (3 large ones) if using fresh
- 2 cups (or three average-size bread slices) bread crumbs
- 4 tablespoons melted butter
- ¼ cup orange juice (fresh or frozen)

Directions

1. In a medium bowl mix sugar, flour, salt, cinnamon and allspice. Set aside.

2. Scald, peel and pit the peaches (if using fresh). Then cut each peach in half, then in six lengthwise slices.

3. Butter an 8-inch round or square pan and spread one cup of bread crumbs on the bottom.

4. Cover with peach slices, pit side down.

5. Spoon on 2 tablespoons of melted butter.

6. Sprinkle on all of the sugar, flour, spice mix and the remaining cup of bread crumbs.

7. Add the final 2 tablespoons of melted butter and orange juice.

8. Bake in the oven at 375 F for 30 minutes or until browned.

9. Serve warm with whipped cream or vanilla ice cream.

 **Barn Cat Cheese Platter**

(serves 4-6)

Ingredients

- one 8 oz wedge of Swiss cheese

- one 8 oz. wedge of Colby cheese

- one 8 oz. wedge of Pepper Jack cheese

- one 8 oz. wedge of Cheddar cheese

- a package of toothpicks

Directions

1. Unwrap the cheese wedges and let sit until soft and room temperature.

2. Slice cheese with a dull knife into 1-inch, bite-size cubes.

3. Stick toothpicks through the top of each piece and arrange on a large platter.

4. Share immediately. No barn cats allowed.

Mrs. Murphy's Famous Chocolate Chip Cookies (about 4 dozen)

Ingredients

- 1 cup (two sticks of butter)
- ¾ cup granulated sugar
- ¾ cup light brown sugar
- 1 teaspoon vanilla extract
- 2 eggs
- 2 ¼ cups all-purpose flour
- 1 teaspoon baking soda
- ½ teaspoon salt
- 1 cup white chocolate chips (any brand)
- 1 cup dark chocolate chips (any brand)

Directions

1. Heat oven to 375 F

2. In a large bowl, use a hand mixer to blend butter, sugar, brown sugar and vanilla until well combined.

3. Add the eggs and beat the mixture more.

4. In a smaller bowl, use a fork to blend the flour, baking soda and salt. Then, add all of this to the large wet mixture and beat until it forms a soft dough.

5. Stir in dark and white chocolate chips with a wooden spoon.

6. Use a regular teaspoon to drop chunks of dough on ungreased cookie sheets.

7. Bake about 10 minutes or until browned.

8. Remove cookies and place on cooling racks.

9. Enjoy and share with others when cooled.

Made in the USA
Coppell, TX
02 December 2020

42777332R00059